ZANY ZOO

WILLIAM WISE

Illustrated by LYNN MUNSINGER

Houghton Mifflin Company Boston 2006

Walter Lorraine Books

Zany Zoo is dedicated

with admiration and affection to my old

and true friend Marilyn Marlow

Walter Lorraine (*wl*) Books

Text copyright © 2006 by William Wise
Illustrations copyright © 2006 by Lynn Munsinger

www.houghtonmifflinbooks.com

Library of Congress Cataloging-in-Publication Data

Wise, William, 1923–
  Zany zoo / by William Wise; illustrated by Lynn Munsinger.
    p. cm.
  Summary: An illustrated, pun-filled collection of short rhymes
about a variety of animals, including Gertrude the good agouti and
Sabrina the carefree snake.
    ISBN-13: 978-0-618-18891-8
    ISBN-10: 0-618-18891-6
[1. Zoo animals—Fiction. 2. Animals—Fiction. 3. Stories in rhyme.]
I. Munsinger, Lynn, ill. II. Title.
    PZ8.3.W743Zan 2006
    [E]—dc22
                                        2005020058
ISBN: 0-618-18891-6
ISBN-13: 978-0-618-18891-8

Printed in Singapore
TWP 10 9 8 7 6 5 4 3 2 1

Daisy

There was a dog named Daisy,
    Who did not care for meat.
In fact, ripe watermelon
    Was what she liked to eat.

Her diet was eccentric
    But not an act of folly.
She loved that juicy fruit because
    She was a melon collie.

Lambert the Lion

Lambert the lion
   Had a bad reputation.
Telling fibs seemed to be
   His chief occupation.
So when he began
   Selling packets of meat,
And swore that his wares
   Were delightful to eat,
Those who knew him just laughed
   And said, "No, we ain't buyin'!
Why should we believe him
   When we know that he's lion!"

Young Yuri, the Yak

Young Yuri, the yak, was quite plucky,
For though he thought yogurt was yucky,
He valiantly ate
What Mom plopped on his plate,
And dreamed of things fried in Kentucky.

The Baseball Elephants

Two young elephants, Kermit and Kit,
Pitched Little League baseball one summer.
Kermit's curve wasn't easy to hit,
And Kit's fastball was really a hummer.

It was strange to see elephants playing,
And to hear them both greeted with cheers,
But it merely confirmed the old saying—
Little pitchers really do have big ears.

Gertrude Was a Good Agouti

Gertrude was a good agouti,
    Who always tried to do her duty.
She did the cooking and the sweeping,
    While sister Grace was upstairs sleeping,
Until a jaguar, for his dinner,
    Devoured Grace, that lazy sinner.
Then Gertrude, forced to dine alone,
    Ate Grace's ice cream, and her own.
For good agoutis, though it hurts,
    Do finally get their just desserts.

Sabrina

Sabrina was a carefree snake,
    An independent spirit
Who loved the sound of laughter
    And the times when she could hear it.

But Sabrina had a boyfriend,
    Who was really very proper,
And when she'd laugh, he'd always frown
    And do his best to stop her.

So Sabrina dumped her boyfriend
    For a garter snake named Willy,
A cheerful lad, who was never sad,
    And told jokes long and silly.

Then Sabrina sang a song of joy,
    And proclaimed herself the victor,
Declaring that she'd never let
    Another beau constrict her.

The Wonder Bat

Young Bradford was a busy bat,
　　Who worked in Muller's Diner.
He served the customers all day
　　And thought no job was finer.

He brought them doughnuts filled with jam,
　　He brought them ham and eggs,
And served the food much faster than
　　A waiter with long legs.

In every sort of circumstance,
　　He served the folks at Muller's,
And always did that wonder bat
　　Come through with flying crullers!

Rob the Raccoon

Rob the raccoon
  Was a pickpocket whiz,
Which meant that your money
  Very soon became his.

He attended parades
  In all kinds of weather,
For he did his best work
  Where folks crowded together.

A slide through your purse,
  A paw in your pocket,
And your money was gone
  With the speed of a rocket.

Yes, packed in with others,
  He found work confining,
But he knew every crowd
  Has a real silver lining.

Harry the Horse

Harry the horse loved a dentist,
　　And so, to her office he went,
Gave her flowers, and said, "I've a toothache!"
　　And considered the money well spent.

But she said, "I'll not treat your toothache!
　　I'm a mare who grew up in the South,
Where you're taught not to listen to strangers
　　Or to look a gift horse in the mouth!"

Pedro the Panda

Pedro the panda
    And five panda pals,
Started dancing the samba,
    With six panda gals.

There were shouts of "Olé!"
    But no neighbors complained
On that festival day,
    When panda-monium reigned.

The Big Nose

I think you'd like to meet the tapir.
Though I can't guess what forces shape her.
Prodigious is her giant nose.
I guess it simply grows and grows.
Yes, she is huge, both nose and muzzle.
The reason, though, remains a puzzle.

Two Terns

Tess, a tern,
  Snapped up a flea,
And gave the prize
  To Tom, her brother.

Then Tom gave Tess
  His clams—all three—
For one good tern
  Deserves another.

Kenneth the Boomer

Kenneth was a "boomer,"
   A towering kangaroo,
And most days he'd greet strangers
   With a friendly "Howdy-do!"

But Kenneth had a temper,
   He was a short-fused lad,
And no one liked to meet him,
   When he was hopping mad.

Lulu

Lulu was a little skunk,
    The oddest one alive.
All the other skunks smelled awful—but
    She smelled of Chanel 5!

Because her scent was lovely,
    They mocked her very name.
So Lulu went to Paris,
    And there found wealth and fame.

For years she lived in style.
    Her chateau was immense.
Which shows that, when it comes to skunks,
    It pays to have good scents.

Young Carlos

Young Carlos was a crocodile,
A species known for strength and guile.
"Of me," he cried, "let all be wary!
I'm the ruler of this estuary!"
Alas, that wasn't strictly true—
A bigger croc soon came in view,
Decided it was time to sup,
And promptly gobbled Carlos up.

Vain Bess

An Indian tigress, whose name was Bess,
Wore nothing in public but native dress.
Her beautiful saris she greatly prized,
While the clothes of foreigners she despised.
Until one unfortunate afternoon,
She got soaking wet in a huge monsoon,
And when it was over, I know you'd agree,
Poor Bess was a real sari sight to see.

A Mouse Named Mary

A mouse named Mary couldn't rest,
   When food was on her mind,
And so she left her little nest,
   To see what she could find.

An open window caught her eye,
   And a cake that looked quite nice!
So in she slipped and, on the sly,
   Purloined a luscious slice!

Then they cheered her daring enterprise,
   Throughout the mouse community,
Where it was said, she'd seized her prize,
   Through a window of opportunity.

A Big Family

Olga the otter
   Was a mother supreme.
She had enough children
   For a large soccer team.

But her kids were so many,
   She sometimes lost track of them,
Till she dressed them in shirts,
   With their names on the back of them.

And they say, after that,
   It was not an illusion,
That they all lived in less
   Than otter confusion.

Wally the Whale

Wally the whale was a playboy,
   A genial and vast bon vivant.
No more fun-loving host or companion
   Could anyone possibly want.

Wally's lifestyle has not been forgotten,
     For it's still said in prose and in rhyme,
When you kick up your heels at a party,
     Then you're having a whale of a time.

Carlotta the Cow

Carlotta the cow
   Was gentle and sweet,
Except on the subject
   Of Good Things to Eat.

Some grass in the pasture
   Was especially delicious,
And exclusively *hers*—
   Till some sheep got ambitious.

They slipped through the fence,
   And started to dine,
When Carlotta came up
   And said, "Clear out! That's MINE!"

So they backed through the fence,
   In a panicky crowd,
And you could say those sheep
   Had been thoroughly cowed.

Doing Shakespeare

A gaggle of geese got together,
    And agreed to do something theatrical.
But since few of them had any talent,
    The decision may have not been too practical.

Still, the costumes were made, and the scenery,
    And Ophelia and Hamlet appeared,
While Queen Gertrude kept preening her feathers,
    And King Claudius honked away through his beard.

But finally the performance was over,
    And in the morning, one critic did say,
After twenty-two years of reviewing,
    He'd at last seen a truly fowl play!

A Real Cool Cat

Kevin was a real cool cat
Who ate too much, and got too fat,
Then fell in love with a gorgeous feline,
And to his closet, he made a beeline.

"This doll," he thought, "does truly please me!
So into my duds I had better squeeze me!"
Then out they went and began to dance,
To spin and leap, to strut and prance.

But Kevin's clothing was much too snug,
And suddenly, as they cut a rug,
His seams all burst, for the world to see
That he'd suffered a social cat-astrophe.

Hope the Hyena

Hope the hyena
Was courageous and plucky.
A fine ballerina,
She at first was unlucky.

For when she appeared
As the Sugar Plum Fairy,
The children all cried
And said she looked scary.

So they switched her to Faust
And the regions infernal.
And now she's a star,
Proving Hope springs eternal.

Charley the Chicken, Who Crossed the Road

Said Charley the chicken,
 "Now what's all this fuss?
Though I *did* cross the road,
 There was no car or bus.

"So over I went,
 And hey-diddle-diddle,
I wound up a famous
 American riddle!"*

* Famous American Riddle:
Question: Why did the chicken cross the road?
Answer: To get to the other side.

Four Rabbits

Basil and Betty,
   Bobbie and Bill,
Were four little rabbits,
   Who lived on a hill.

Each day they ate garlic,
   Which grew round the place,
And when Mr. Fox chased them,
   They blew fumes in his face.

Then Mr. Fox choked—
   It was such a fine jape!—
While those four clever rabbits
   Made their hares' breath escape.